THE KiTTEN THAT CLUCKED

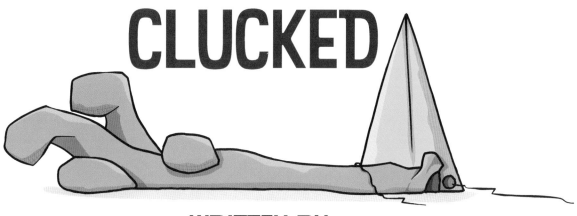

WRITTEN BY
PAUL PENNiNGTON
ILLUSTRATED BY
MATT LEAKE

FOR DORiS

**Two kittens, named Bob and May,
lived on a farm and played all day.**

Come on, let's play hide and seek.
You count to five and do not peek.

One and two, three, four, and five.
I'm coming now, you'd better hide.

Where ever shall I start to look?
In every cranny and every nook.

Let's look in that rotten log.

**May keeps on searching
high and low.**

She can't find Bob, where did he go?

Maybe the pond, let's try our luck.

That's not Bob, it's just a duck!

May scratches her head in such a muddle,

but all she can see is a mucky puddle.

Let's search the tractor and its load.

That's not Bob,
it's just a toad!

**May searches and searches to no avail.
She looks in pots and rusty pails.**

Let's look in the
chicken pen.

That's not Bob, it's just a hen!

May is tired and
close to quitting.

One last try, let's find that kitten.

Let's search for Bob back in the house.
Ha, caught you Bob, you're not a mouse!

Clever May, she is the winner.
Just as well, it's time for dinner.

THE END.

Printed in Great Britain
by Amazon